THE CIRCUS

WRITTEN BY AMELIA HARRIS

Dedication
I'd like to dedicate my very first book to my mum, Dionne.
Without her, I wouldn't have had the courage to follow my dreams.
My love of books first started with her love for them.
Thank you.

Chapter One

A great roar rang through the crowd, clapping, cheering, applause. Jasmine, once again, had stunned the crowed below with her world famous performance. Each time they'd think she'd ended her act, but, they were wrong. One final stunt would seem to prove fatal, until she'd wow the audience and prove them all wrong. Hanging off a single wire, Jasmine would swing back and forth until her feet could touch the roof of the circus tent, her small but slender body would twist and turn, often leaving the audience with a churning stomach. Then, crash, she'd seem to fall thirty feet to her death where she'd produce a hurdle of turns before landing perfectly on her feet each time. A standing ovation would occur where flowers, money and presents would come flying into the centre ring.
"Jasmine Ladies and Gents" a booming voice would sound as a tall man with a cane and top hat would appear from behind the red velvet curtain. The clapping and cheering from the audience would grow louder as Jasmine left the centre ring and made her way back to her dressing room. She'd slip out of her dress and tights and into a pair of checkered trousers and black top. She'd slip her teddy bear jacket on top and grab her bag before heading out of the circus. She'd done it, once again, a successful performance completed.

Her walk home was calm and quiet walk, often, she'd opt for the back routes leaving her not to be disturbed by passers by or fans, although, she never liked to call them that. Being approached by spectators was a regular occurrence for Jasmine. Normally it would be gifts, letters, flowers and on a more regular occasion, just a congratulatory conversation. Walking on the quiet route, left Jasmine happier, she'd never feel unsafe or open to unwelcome visitors, but tonight told a different tale. This night seemed darker than normal, fewer stars seemed to light up the nights sky and the air seemed to be colder than usual. Tonight, Jasmine found herself turning around on a regular basis, almost as if she were being followed. A couple of rats scurried across her path whilst a set of foxes seemed to howl at her as she passed. Then...
"Jasmine!" A man shouted at her, but not in anger or for her attention, but in recognition. Of course this wasn't out of the ordinary for her, but this man seemed to know her personally, although, she had no idea where from. The tall and slender man was a few yards behind her, she upped her speed and swiftly left the gloomy street, doing her best not to draw attention to herself.

Getting home was a relief. The warm and comfortable feeling swarmed her body as she took off her shoes and placed her bag beside the front door. Her parents were asleep already so the house was engulfed in darkness, she switched on the lights and lit up her surrounds. Jasmine switched on the evening news, sat herself down on the sofa and somehow, managed to fall asleep from the long day she'd had within minutes.
A few hours later, she was awoken by a series of small taps that seemed to be coming from the back of the house. Her security light wasn't turned on but a definite noise was present. It spooked her but seem to phase her as such. She managed to drag herself off the sofa and clamber her way towards the kitchen which was placed at the back of the house, switching on the security light, she rubbed her eyes and managed to focus on what seemed to be a small handwritten envelope and a rose placed just outside the backdoor. Alarmed but not scared, Jasmine cautiously opened the backdoor, grabbed at the letter and shut the backdoor in one fell swoop, leaving her scared as to if she'd woken her parents up. Silence filled the house as Jasmine made her way back to the living room

where the TV was purely static. She switched it off and sat down, placing the mysterious note and flower in front of her on the coffee table. She pondered for a minute or so. Thoughts were racing through her head as she questioned whether she should take the plunge and open the letter or leave it and ignore it. Getting fan mail was so normal for her but to get something delivered to her door, that was strange, especially at night. Something twinged in her body, something willed her to open the strange envelope. Reaching out her hand, she grabbed the envelope and prised it open, not giving herself a chance to change her mind. Upon opening the letter, she found a hand written note reading:

'My dearest Jasmine,

I have watched you perform plenty of times. You're my favourite act at the circus and you're the reason I go back. I'd love to meet you one day in person. We're meant to be together. You're my soul mate. One day we'll meet. I love you.

Lots of love,

Your soul mate'

A cold shiver ran down her spine. A tingle ran up her arms as she realised this man had hand delivered this note to her house. To her door. She tucked the note to the back of a draw upstairs in her bedroom and decided to forget all about it. It was early in the morning so Jasmine made the decision to go to bed and ignore the events that had just occurred.

Jasmine woke up with her parents clambering out of bed. She turned herself over and took a long hard look at the clock, 7am, too early. Although her parents assumed she attended university, she never had to be up and out of the door before her parents had to leave for work. They were both lawyers, the sort of lawyers you had to be hired for. The rich kind. Jasmine was their only child and a lot was riding on her shoulders to follow in their footsteps and make them proud, achieving what they achieved and more. Normally Jasmine would be able to get herself back to sleep, she was lazy in that sense but the work she was achieving each night left her tired and exhausted so she had every right to be. Today was different. She couldn't forget about the night before. She couldn't even force herself to ignore it all. It was like the letter was screaming at her from her bedside draw, like it was calling her name in a whispered tone. She stared for a good few minutes at the draw, she didn't want to open it again, she didn't want to stir all of it up and embrace all the worry and panic, but she couldn't help but take a peek. As soon as she took hold of the letter, all of her thoughts from the night before came flooding back. All of the fear, confusion, anger. Everything. Then her mind took her back to the man in the street, he had found her way home, could it be him? Could that have been the man? Jasmine was seriously into real crime shows, none of that made up nonsense, but it made her more aware. After the previous events, she decided to change her route home, making sure she'd pass security camera's and pass through the public. That way, she'd be in less danger.

A few hours later and Jasmine was getting ready for work, her dress, a pink tutu and fitted leotard with some skin coloured tights today. She fitted them all into her bag along with her purse, keys and phone. The letter still loomed in her mind but her head was mostly full of work and her act. It was her favourite part of the day. Jasmine lived in Newcastle, there weren't many circus' around which meant that her work, where she worked, they were a family. They were close knit and they'd all look out for each other.

Getting into work today felt like a relief but something seemed strange. Something seemed off. There was a solemn atmosphere in the tent today, a sense of despair and desperation was pouring around the building like a foul smell. There was a crowd gathering in the middle of the ring, a circle of the main acts having an important conversation about god knows what. Jasmine walked straight past and into her dressing room, one of the ballerinas walked past and stopped in her tracks, peering at Jasmine from the doorway.

"I'm so sorry Jasmine" the ballerina, who's name was Lucy, was hovering at the doorway. A single tear trickled down her cheek like a diamond falling slowly.

"Sorry about what Lucy?" Confusion. That's all that was running through her veins, pure confusion.

"Oh. Graham. The ring man. He died. Murdered. Right here. God awful sight it was" Lucy handed Jasmine his cane and top hat before giving a false smile and leaving to go back to her dressing room. Jasmine was left holding the top hat and cane in the middle of the room, she slumped into the sofa at the side of the room. 'Murdered' she thought. After what had happened the night before, could it be connected? Who would murder Graham?!

Obviously there was no show today. The news of the ring masters death spread quickly, like an infection getting a hold of the body. Jasmine's body was trembling inside, the thought of what had happened the previous night engulfed her mind. She could tell her parents, they were lawyers of course, but that meant telling them she worked in a circus. They'd without a doubt disapprove of her choice of career. No. She couldn't do that. She had to deal with this her own way. Jasmine Stayed slumped on the sofa for another half an hour. She couldn't shake all the thoughts racing through her head. She couldn't take her bright green eyes off the cane and top hat. She couldn't shake the feeling that she was being watched. That she had someone looking at her all of the time, like a camera following her around.

It must have been half eight by the time she decided to head home, it was summer so it was still light, but the prospect of walking home alone seemed daunting. Seemed scary. Nobody was left in the circus tent but Jasmine by this time, she'd found it hard to come to terms with what had happened today. However, she still decided to stick to the new route, even with a clouded head.

The air outside was warm and inviting, the sun was setting and fewer people seemed to be out. The smell of food was poignant, pubs were crawling with people, empty glasses once filled with alcohol was now tipped over on the outside tables. Men shouting and stumbling out of bars almost bumped into Jasmine on her way past. A twenty minute walk proved to be easy for Jasmine today. Nobody shouting. Nobody asking her questions or asking for photos. Just easy. Getting home from a long day was rewarding but getting on with normal tasks proved to be the hard part. As she turned on the news, pictures of Graham were plastered across the screen and the radio was the same. Interviews with the police chief and pictures of the circus tent was everywhere. Then, she saw something she really didn't want to. They carried out his body. Jasmine was always sensitive but at the same time, nothing would get in her way. The death of someone she loved so dearly, wasn't going to stop her from getting what she wanted and the justice Graham deserved.

A few days later Jasmine decided to attend his funeral. Everyone from the circus was going and in true tradition, they all wore their costumes to honour him. Ballerinas, ventriloquists, Acrobats and of course Jasmine in her leotard and tutu. On top of his coffin sat his top hat and cane alongside a wreath and his photo. The board standing to the side of the church held a notice, almost a remembrance of him and his life.

'After many years of service at the circus, we're here today to pay our respects to a beloved man, colleague, father, brother and uncle. He'll be missed by all and loved forever.'

Jasmine stood and stared at the board, more photos of him were placed beneath it and more flowers were laid around. As the music played, people started to gather in their seats ready for the service to commence.

The service lasted for maybe an hour and throughout, sobbing could be heard from almost everyone but Jasmine, she couldn't stop thinking about the letter she'd found a few days before. It was still playing on her mind and almost everywhere she went, everywhere she turned, she found herself peering around corners and checking to see who she s with. Who knew one piece of paper could make her feel so uneasy.

As Jasmine got home, she found herself wanting to do nothing but go to bed. It had been a long day full of despair and sorrow. Sadness and loss.
The sun set and the events of the day slid away with it, Jasmine climbed into bed and shut her eyes, shutting out the stress from the day.

Chapter Two

Detective Chief Inspector Josh Dixon stormed into the office and slammed the doors open so loud, the whole building shuddered leaving several fresh faced officers shivering in their boots.

"Who? Who killed him?! Come on. We must have a lead by now" Dixon was wafting paper around the place. Documents in his hand, bank statements, birth certificate. Anything relating to Graham Sammy, the ring master. Several young officers looked blankly at the DCI. He waved his hand in the air giving them all daring looks.

"Nothing?! C'mon guys!" He huffed and walked over to the board standing in the middle of the room. He took a magnet and pinned Graham's photo onto the board, writing his name underneath in a green marker.

Joshua Dixon was an older man, grey hair seeping through the roots of his dyed hair. He stood and stared at the board in the officer, like he was waiting for the answers to present themselves to him, like they were about to jump out at him. Nothing. He huffed and took himself off to his office where he fell into his chair and spun around, facing the back wall. A knock at the door startled the DCI.

"Sir, I checked through his phone records, he called one number four times the night he died. It's a pay as you go so no way to trace it unfortunately" a young girl was standing at his door, older, mid thirties with long dark brown hair. He huffed again. This seemed to be a regular occurrence recently.

"Friends, work colleagues. Do they all check out?" He pulled his face, the face he does when he's trying to come up with the answer himself but can't, kind of like a squint.

"Yeah. Everyone checks out" the female officer walked out of the room and back to her desk. No new leads. Graham was a liked man, no enemies. No enemies himself he thought.

"SARAH! Check to see if any of the other performers have known enemies!" He grabbed his coat and swiftly but calmly ran out the door.

Dixon arrived back at the crime scene, the circus tent. He walked back into the centre ring where the ring masters body had been discovered earlier in the day. The blood stains still presented themselves through the mats and sand that lay on the floor. He lifted up the crime scene tape and stood towering over where Graham once lay. He walked around in a circle, making a humming noise every few seconds to show he was pondering, to show he was thinking. He tapped the papers from before on his chin and stopped in his tracks. He lowered the papers and sifted through them.

'Graham Jack Sammy. Found dead at the circus tent where he performed as the ring master. No next of kin.

Died from a single stab wound to the heart. The blade still present.

Most likely a form of symbolism.

Being stabbed in the heart symbolises the end of love.

Other injuries present. Bruises to the torso shows the man was beaten.
Ropes tied around his ankles suspended him from the ceiling'

Dixon read over those notes a few times before asking himself the most important question he could in that moment. 'How did they suspend him from the ceiling?'
They'd have to know what they were doing. Be strong, slender and flexible. Maybe more than one person. Could a woman do this? Maybe a man? One, two or three people?

Questions filled his head like a swarm of flies infesting a room. Questions began to get jumbled in with answers and notes. He huffed once again and shook his head.

Then the curtain swayed slightly. Like a gust of wind moved it but all the doors were closed. His eyes were fixed on the read velvet curtain, he didn't move an inch. Then he saw a small pair of eyes peering at him from behind. A small boy who darted away when he saw Dixon staring back at him.

"You ok there son" Dixon was standing facing the crime scene with his head bent to the side.

"Yes sir" the boy was no older then six. His short brown hair left him looking paler than a normal boy of his age would be. He started to walk out of the curtain and towards Dixon.

"Are you the police?" He was small, could have easily been missed.

"Yes I am. Can I help?" Dixon lowered himself down to the boys level. Crouching, he became level with his eyes.

"My names William sir. But everyone calls me Billy. Little Billy. I saw him. I saw the man. He was hurt, wondering and stumbling around the place. He couldn't stand. He looked drunk"

"Graham you mean?" He was astounded, Billy could have been killed too.

"Yes sir. He was screaming and shouting... at nobody, he was on his own" Billy skipped off into the red velvet curtain, leaving DCI Dixon crouched in the centre ring. He'd learnt some valuable information.

Dixon waltzed back into the office and wafted paper in the air, the door slammed shut behind him.

"Drugged. He was drugged" Dixon pinned the toxicology report into the board and tapped it before repeating his earlier words.

"I met a young boy who told me Graham was stumbling and shouting at nothing, at nobody. So I checked the toxicology report which indicated he had drugs in his system. Specifically. Poison" The room fell silent, you could have heard a pin drop. It was as if nobody knew what to do from that moment onwards. It wasn't something they'd seen before, all the officers were too young. But not Dixon. He raced back into his office where his grabbed his phone and started dialling. He phoned every college, university or school within the local area, starting with science specialists. This gave him a clear picture on students, what someone would need to make someone see things and if any equipment may be missing. To his luck, the local school came up trumps. St Evergreen's were missing several pieces of equipment, it had been reported weeks back and had shown up no trace.

Dixon was still baffled by who Graham may have called that night. Who would he want to speak to four times in one evening. Each call lasted almost exactly a minute and Graham was the one hanging up and calling back each time. All his family checked out, friends seemed to as well, so this must have been someone he hardly knew. An acquaintance if you like. Someone he must have met in passing. Dixon scribbled down some notes on the case file and closed it shut. He picked up the brown file and slid it into his desk draw, he locked it shut and laid back in his chair. He put his arms under his head and swung around, leaving his back facing the large window in his office. It was like he'd hit a brick wall, there was no path he could pursue, no obvious route out.

Sarah burst into Dixon's office letting the door swing open and hit the wall, leaving a dent from the handle.

"Another.... another one..." she huffed and sighed as she struggles to catch her breath, she'd just run up three flights of stairs and through the office. She was holding a tablet in her hand which she placed on Dixon's desk after stumbling over to him.

"Sarah. Stop. Catch your breath. What do you mean another one?" Dixon had shot up by this point, his head and neck poised like a meerkat.

"There's been another murder. The same happened, a man was stabbed and hung from a ridiculously high ceiling" Dixon swiped through the crime scene photos. The man in the images looked strong and like he'd fight back.

"Was he in the same line of work?" His eyes darted between Sarah and the crime scene photos in front of him on the tablet. Sarah looked at him, paused and gave a small smile.

"No... he wasn't" Dixon's eyes shot up at her, suddenly, it all started to make sense and started to piece itself together. The man from the most recent murder was dressed as a ring man. A top hat tied to his head with elastic, the red waistcoat and tail wrapped around him. A cane glued to his hand.

"So this killer, the murders, they're centred around the circus. Around the ring man" Dixon and Sarah nodded at each other and walked out of his office. Finally, Dixon had his path to go down, his hidden route that he so desperately needed to find.

The crime scene offered hope of new leads in the case. Dixon was wandering around the body still hanging by the ceiling, the knife still wedged in his back. The coroner arrived just after Dixon, a woman with short black hair and a leather jacket. She walked over to the body to start taking a look. Dixon walked over to shake her hand.

"Dixon. I'm the DCI on this case" she reached back out to shake his hand.

"Alice. I'm the coroner and I'm here to examen the body" she smiled and walked over. Dixon gave a small run after her.

"First thoughts. Anything standing out?" She looked back around at him and then looked over to the body.

"Well. They'd have to be strong. The knife. There's no blood, this either means they cleaned the body down or it was done post mortem. They were stabbed after they died" Dixon looked slowly around at Alice. He gave a small and slow nod and waved at the officers.

"Lower the body" he shouted at five young officers waiting for the go ahead to get the victim down.

After five long minutes, the victim was finally on the floor, he was laid on his front to prevent further damage with the knife. Alice walked over, slipped some gloves on and bent down. She went straight to the knife wound to properly examen it, undoing the jacket with care and ease. Dixon also slipped some gloves on and crouched down beside her.

"So? Anti mortem or post mortem?" He touched the mans back to see how deep it went.

"Post. He was definitely dead first" Alice had her glasses on by this point, she had her full kit laid out on the floor.

"So? Now here's the real question, what killed him and was it the same for Graham Sammy?" Alice once again smiled as Dixon finished asking his question.

"I'll get back to you on that" Dixon once again smiled and walked off, lifting the police tape over his head. He ripped off his gloves as he strutted back to his car and headed towards the office.

Once he was back at is office he found himself pacing back and forth. Why this man? Why was he killed?

Dixon could see it all had something to do with the circus, but what? Five minutes later Sarah knocked on the door and came in holding two pieces of paper in her hands.

"His name is Madden sir, Alex Madden. He was a security guard at a bar two streets away from here. Today was his last shift before he left for Canada" Dixon shook his head, not at Sarah but in sorrow and disgust. His last day before he starts his new life and he dies. Tragic. Sarah left Dixon pacing in his office again. A security guard? Why would they kill a security guard? Of course Dixon had looked at the prospect it might have just been coincidence or wrong place wrong time but Mr Alex Madden could have fought back, he could have taken on his killer.

For the rest of the day Dixon was sifting through CCTV footage of Madden's day to see if he could piece together where he may have met them. Once again, Sarah then came through the office door.
"Sir, he too had made a handful of phone calls to an untraceable number…" Dixon was baffled. This just fuelled the mystery and added to the pressure he had on his shoulders from the media, from his boss and the family and friends of the victims. Who could these calls be to?

Chapter Three

Jasmine woke up with a start, the events of the previous night still loomed in her head. That's all she could think about. The sun was shining through the cracks in her blinds and resting itself onto her face. Gleaming through the cracks in her eyes. She squinted and rubbed her eyes. Jasmine sat up slowly, pushing herself up with her arms. Jasmine decided to sit there for a minute, she peered out of the window and looked out at the new day ahead, focusing on what prospects it could bring, what might happen. Her thoughts still focused on Graham though. Then it hit her, she had no job right now, the circus of course wouldn't resume until the funeral or until after it was no longer a crime scene. So... what to do with her day?

A knock at the door startled her, the banging sent her heart into the pit of her stomach. Jasmine's bedroom stood at the front of the house, she made her way over to the window to find another note sitting on her doorstep with a white rose to accompanying it this time. Shivers were sent down her spin. A sickening feeling engulfed her body and sent her trembling body cashing to the floor. The feeling of being followed, a note, Graham dead, another man dead and another note... someone was definitely watching her, but why?
After a solid five minutes, Jasmine found the courage within her to open her door and take the note in. Jasmine cautiously made her way downstairs, her legs shaking with every step, she opened the door slowly and peered out of the small crack to see if anyone may be there. Once she'd seen it was empty, Jasmine reached out her arm and lifted the note along with the rose and slammed the door shut again. Locking it shut, Jasmine slid down the door and placed herself onto the floor with the note resting on her knee's. She carefully opened the envelope and slid out the note which was yet again, hand written. It read:

' Jasmine,
    Me and you were meant to be together. By now I'm sure you've heard about the two killings... naturally they were to protect you. Those people may have seemed close, but they were hurting you, surrounding you and not letting you out. You needed freedom and I've helped given it to you. We'll meet one day my dearest Jasmine. You're my soul mate and you own my heart. I'll see you at the circus when they re-open. I promise.
    Lots of love
    M.W'

The note this time seemed to be more personal. It seemed closer to home and ultimately, seemed to pose more of a threat. Jasmine knew exactly what she had to do, she had to take the notes to the police. They had to know that whoever was killing these people, was a dangerous person, someone who wasn't planning on stopping anytime soon. Jasmine just had to find the courage and motivation inside her to actually leave the house and go to the police. Then the thought of her parents popped into her head. They could be hurt, this person, this sick and deluded person was killing anyone she cared about, anyone she loved and they couldn't be next.
Jasmine clambered up and turned to face the door when it dawned on her. Someone else she loved must have been killed. A name hadn't been released yet but it must be someone she knew. Without hesitation this time, she swung the front door open, gripping tight-

ly onto the notes and made her way towards her car. She kept the pace quick and swift and once she was in her car, she locked it tight. Jasmine clung onto the steering wheel tight and didn't let go, she held her breath and once she realised she was safe, released a sigh of relief.

When she entered the police station it was warm and inviting. The smell of sugary snacks looked in the air and the looming stench of stale coffee surrounded her. Jasmine's hands were trembling causing the notes in her hand to shake uncontrollably. A police officer sitting at the reception desk noticed Jasmine and lowered her glasses, peering over just enough she could see the confused look on her face. Jasmine noticed her looking and ran over, looking behind her and noticing every aspect of her surroundings. Who she was with, entrances, exits. All of it was being clocked in her mind.
"Hi. I need to speak to someone. I've been getting notes and..." The woman at the counter put her hand up and stopped Jasmine speaking. She gave Jasmine an understanding look and said,
"Say no more.... I'll get someone out" Jasmine had no idea how she knew what was happening, or even if she did know at all. She spun around on the spot and sat herself down in the corner, away from any windows and doors.

Two hours had passed before anyone came to see Jasmine, her left leg was shaking in the spot and her fingernails had been worn down drastically from her biting them. A young officer came out, dark brown hair, suit all buttoned up and perfectly presented. He smiled gracefully to show perfect white and straight teeth.
"Jasmine isn't it? With me" Cautiously jasmine followed him, she peered around every corner they went down and made sure to shut every door behind her before carrying on. He sat Jasmine down in an office and he left the room.
Another twenty minutes passed before an officer walked through the door. It was DCI Dixon. He was carrying papers in one hand, neatly placed in a folder and in the other hand, a coffee which had been sipped intermittently.
"So, I hear you want to speak to someone about these letters you've been getting" Dixon leaned over the table, his elbows placed on the table and his back arched which he'd clearly regret later. Jasmine looked astonished. She hadn't said anything to the receptionist. How did they know?!
"Sorry sir. I don't mean to pry but I don't understand, how do you know... I didn't say anything to the woman downstairs?" Dixon sighed and slid back into his chair. He placed his fingertips together and rested his elbows on the arms of the chair.
"Someone came in this morning and handed in a photo of you. They said you may come in but that if you do, we should call them. That you were missing and they were worried."
Again, Dixon gave a sigh. This time he reached for his bad smelling coffee and sipped it slowly before placing it down on the table with a dissatisfied look on his face.
"What?! No. He's stalking me. I work at the same circus as Graham. He said he killed them...both" Jasmine had this panicked look on her face. Her eyes darting back and forth. Dixon shot up in his seat. His eyes glaring at Jasmine and his tone turned from boredom to panic.
"You mean to tell me, that they man I met earlier, the man who handed in your photo and wrote you these letters, is the killer?!" Dixon realised this was his big chance. His big break in the case. The biggest lead he'd had the entire time he case was open. He reached out his hand and waited patiently for Jasmine to hand him the letters. She did so willingly and watched DCI Dixon read every word thoroughly before getting up from his seat and leaving. Jasmine was left sitting in Dixon's Office. The worry grew in her mind as she realised that even in the police station, Jasmine just wasn't safe. This man could be anybody. She was completely and utterly alone and had not a soul to turn to.

People kept popping into her head. A performer, a spectator, a friend… it could be anyone and she'd have no idea. She wished and hoped that she could lock herself in this office forever and the man who did this would get bored and leave her alone. That she'd get rid of him and finally, Jasmine could be safe.

Chapter Four

Dixon was still reading as he left the office. He bumped into several inanimate objects before taking off his glasses and sticking the notes onto the board. A crowd of officers gathered around and started to read the notes for themselves. Some squirming at the notes, some commenting on how cringe worthy the wording was and others just staring at the letters in disbelief.

"Sarah. I want CCTV from the reception from all of this morning. Then look at the CCTV from the circus again but this time, focus on anyone who pays too much attention to our Jasmine here" Sarah nodded and raced off to go and start the verbal to do list that she'd just been given.

It took maybe ten minutes to gather any CCTV from the morning. Relatively quick for that kind of information but seeing as it was CCTV from the police station itself, it made perfect sense. Dixon and Sarah stood in a small tech room with five computer screens all arched around the technician who was controlling the images. Dixon and Sarah were sitting either side and started to watch the clips from the time frame Jasmine had given him earlier. They fast forwarded the clips to around 10:50am and stared to watch who was coming in and out. After finding no suspects who were already on their database, Dixon made the decision to bring in Jasmine and see if she recognised anybody who may be of interest. Dixon walked back into his office to find Jasmine staring out the window, he swung the door open and leant his body in. Jasmine jumped, her heart able to be heard two streets over. You could see the tears starting to form in her eyes but she soon stopped herself.

"Sorry Jasmine Hun, I didn't mean to startle you. We need you to come and see if you recognise anyone on the CCTV from earlier" Jasmine gave an insecure nod and followed Dixon. His head was a mess. All of these thoughts flooded his mind and all these questions stared to present themselves. He started to get caught up in this case, he was so determined to catch this killer, Dixon started to feel a personal connection rising. He knew it was wrong so he pushed it to the back of his mind.

Once they were in the IT room, Dixon sat Jasmine down in the seat he was originally sitting in. He placed his right arm around the top of it and spoke into her ear.

"Just let me know if you see anyone you recognise, even just in passing" again, Jasmine gave an insecure and unconvinced nod but looked at the footage anyway. It started to play, frame by frame, second by second, you could see the stress, tension and panic creep across Jasmine's face. What happens if she didn't recognise anyone, how long could this continue for?!

Then, she saw him. Although, she didn't quite know what to think. It made sense though, how they'd be able to turn up at her door unnoticed, why the police didn't question it, why it wouldn't feel out of place seeing him at the circus. Questions raced through her head. A flood of emotions spread across her face, making her look more unpredictable than the British weather. Her father... Jasmine had seen her father.

"You see someone?" Dixon peered at Jasmine, waiting for her answer. As the silence grew, Sarah started to peer at Jasmine herself and even the technician started to question why she was so quiet. Jasmine wasn't really sure how to answer. Does she say something and drop her *own* dad in it? Or does she say nothing and confront him herself? Then, in a split second, Jasmine had made up her mind. She shook her head and

Dixon lead her out of the room and into his office. Jasmine has decided she'd confront her mum. She wasn't close to either of her parents but talking to her mum seemed like the best option.

Once they were both sat down, Dixon was handed another foul smelling coffee which, again, he sipped intermittently. He meant back and folded his arms.

"Are you ok to go home, I'll get an officer to walk you to your car and check it out, but would you like an escort?" Dixon waited for Jasmine to say something. Her mind was wrapped in what she'd just seen. She looked up at DCI Dixon with wide eyes and gave a subtle smile.

"I'm ok..." no more words would come out of her mouth. The shock, the disappointment, the worry, it could all be seen on her face, but Dixon knew he couldn't make her say anything. He walked jasmine out to the waiting room and walked back out to the main board.

"How'd it go sir?" A young female officer with flowing brown hair and big blue eyes had walked up and stood right next to him. He took a deep breath and sighed.

"Back to square one..." he gave her a small smile, full of disappointment and took himself off to his office to sulk. All of the officers knew he was too invested in this case but there was this element to it that clung onto him and just wouldn't let him go.

Back in his office he stood and looked at the chair that Jasmine was once sat in, he had this urge to solve this case and help her regain her life. There was something about Jasmine that seemed familiar. Maybe she reminded him of himself but one thing was certain, Dixon knew Jasmine just wasn't safe.

With one fell swoop, Dixon swung his arms across his desk and threw all of the files, pens, paper, mugs and coasters onto the floor. He let out a great roar of anger which sent the whole office into a frenzy. Everyone looked at him but once Dixon had noticed, she shut his blinds and remained in the office till nightfall.

Chapter Five

It took maybe three hours for Jasmine to get home that night. Not because of traffic or
because she lived too far away, but because she didn't necessarily want to go home. It
was like a shield around her house stopping her from getting anywhere near it. Thoughts
swirled around in her head and took over her mind. She couldn't physically think of anything else. Finally, she managed to drive her car into the driveway and park it, although, it
did take her another twenty minutes to actually get out of the car and into the house.
When she finally did get out of her car and into the house, she was greeted by her mother
in the living room watching an episode of her favourite show on TV whilst sipping a coffee
out of a pristine white mug.
"Hi sweetheart! Have you seen this episode. It's an interesting one!" Jasmine just stood in
awe of her mother. How could she not know how much of a creep her husband was being?!
"Urh Yeah... last night. Where's dad?" She watched as her mum took another sip of coffee and then placed it onto the mirrored coaster sitting on the Ikea coffee table.
"No honey. Not since this morning... why?" Jasmine let out a sigh of relief and sat next to
her mother. She took a deep breath and explained everything that had happened in the
last week. She explained all about the murders and the notes and the police station today. Her mum looked at her., smiled a little in one corner and blinked a few times.
"Jasmine. I know. I know what he did. See, truth is. I like you. I do. I love you so much but
the truth is... You're... well, not adopted. Stolen I guess" a sickening feeling ran up Jasmine's spine. She shot up from her seat and took a long hard stare at her mother. The one
she loved and thought she knew. All sorts of emotions ran through her body, fear, anger,
disappointment, love. Jasmine ran towards the door but as soon as she reached it,
stopped. Her heart was ponding in her chest like someone banging on a wooden door.
Jasmine turned around and said one word,
"Why?" Jasmine stood in the doorway to the lounge and stared at the woman she though
she loved, the woman she thought loved her. Again, her mother gave this creepy smile,
only appearing at one corner of her mouth.
"You were so perfect. So precious... and your mother just left you there, crying. I though,
she's not paying attention, she's with that man she called your father, I'll look after you
better than she obviously can, so I took you" a sickening feeling rose in Jasmine's body.
Her mother yet again sat back, switched the TV back on and just ignored everything that
had just been said. Jasmine couldn't move off the spot. She couldn't bring herself to
leave the place she was standing in. So many questions. So many things she could say.
But she left for the door and somehow knew, she was never ever coming back.

Jasmine started up her engine and just drove. In her head, she had no idea where she
was going but somehow, her instincts took her to the police station. She parked in the
police parking, getting yelled at by several officers, she stormed through the main door
behind a young officer leaving for the day and barged her way into Dixon's office. Dixon
shot up with a fright. It looked like he'd been sleeping. Drool was sliding down his face.
Jasmine stood in the doorway, it was the first time in a long time she felt safe. She didn't
ever want to leave this office.
"Jasmine?!" Dixon stood and stared at her whilst she stared to tear up. Water trickled
from her face like diamonds falling into the sea.
"It was my dad on the tape earlier and my mum just told me she kidnapped me" then all
the bottled up emotion came out. Jasmine started sobbing, water ran down her face like

a waterfall. Her face went red and soon she started to feel anger and hate. Her mum, her dad, the real ones, who were they and was she missed?

Officers barged into the Walters home to find Mrs Walters sat on the sofa watching static on her TV. White noise filled the room as two officers grabbed her from her seat and hauled her up and into handcuffs. The whole time, she said with her eyes wide open and a sinister grin spread from ear to ear.

Mr Walters was found at work. He was sat at his desk looking over case files from a case he'd just finished. Again, the police went either side and hauled him up and into handcuffs. He didn't of quietly. He huffed and sighed as he was dragged out of his offie in front of his work colleges. He was repeating the same words.
"What's this about? I haven't done anything. Im a lawyer!" The police did nothing but ignore his arrogance. They knew he was a crook. They knew he needed to be brought in and the offers there with him didn't want to say anything that could aggravate such a violent an deluded man.

Dixon handed Jasmine a cup of tea and sat opposite her in his office. He'd written all of it down and had Sarah follow up on all of the information she'd given him. Soon enough, Mr and Mrs Walters were being walked through the station in handcuffs whilst surrounded by four officers. Jasmine watched as they were walked past the office and started sobbing again.
"What happens now?" Jasmine couldn't bring herself to look up at Dixon. Her eyes stayed fixated on the empty cup she was holding. She had so many questions, so many thoughts and not one she could actually bring herself to say.
"Well we look at missing persons, see if anything matches. We also interview those two out there and see what they have to say" Dixon stood up, patted jasmine on the shoulder and left the room. He gave no explanation as to where he was going but jasmine could imagine. He must be going to watch the interviews, see if she was telling the truth. Maybe he thought she was actually the murderer and they did all of this together or she was trying to get rid of her own parents. Maybe she should leave. Leave before she found out what he thought of her. No, she had nothing to hide. Jasmine stayed seated in the office for what felt like forever. Well, two hours was a long time. With everything that had happened, she just knew that the best place for her was in this office, in this police station. It was the only place she truly felt safe. She couldn't go home, her so called parents were there. If Jasmine left the building, she's risk running into the man she called her father, he could be anywhere right now and he could get to her in anyway he saw fit.

Questions loomed in her mind, after a long day, she decided to picture what her real mother could be like. Tall, short, blonde, brunette, kind or scary. Then, she remembered everything she missed with her. The laughter and the tears. The adventures she could have had with her mum. The woman she though she loved had snatched it all from Jasmine in a matter of seconds, a split decision that cost Jasmine a mum and it had cost her mother a lifetime of pain, sorrow and regret.

Her dad. Jasmine imagined him to be tall with dark brown eyes and dark brown hair. He was strong and kept the whole family safe from any danger they may encounter. He was proud to call himself her father and proud to have his wife, her mother standing beside him.

The next was just pure speculation. Brothers and sisters. She could have loads or she could have none. Jasmine pictured having an older brother and younger sister. Why? She didn't know. Maybe that was a dream of hers but one thing was for sure, she was going to love them all no matter what.

Chapter Six

Dixon had made his way down to missing persons. He walked into a room full of posters and images of all sorts of people. Young, old, girls, boys. There must have been at least one hundred people plastered onto this wall. *Have you seen me?* And *Missing!* Were repeated several times above the photos of people who didn't even know someone was missing them, some may be dead, some alive, but all loved. Dixon walked up to the office stood at the back of the room. He waded through a mound of officers who were scurrying around like ants. He gave a loud knock on the door and entered. An older female officer was sat in the chair, her glasses perched on the tip of her nose and her suit looked perfectly ironed and clean. Then she smiled.
"Josh!" She jumped up from her squeaky leather chair and leaped over to give him a hug. Dixon had forgot until now but she had trained him before he landed the role as a DCI in the same syndicate.
"Ma'am" Dixon gave a brief nod before she sat back down and smiled yet again.
"Sue, please. What can I do you for?" She did the same as Dixon did. She sat back in her chair and folded her arms waiting for him to start talking.
"I have a girl downstairs. She's nineteen, her parents just told her she'd been kidnapped and her supposed father is the main suspect in the killings that have been happening recently" Sue knew this was the most interesting case she'd been involved in for a while. More often than not it was the same stereotypical scenario. Someone goes missing and they turn up at a friends house a few hours after claiming their phone was dead. Most just looking for publicity. She only cared about the real cases. The genuine ones. She gave a nod and asked Dixon to follow her into another small room labelled 'Archives'. Again, she smiled.
"Have a look through these boxes. They're labelled with the year and if they were under three, four to sixteen and so on. They're also done by gender. Hopefully it won't be too hard" Sue left and strutted back to her office, her heals making the whole room shake as she left because it echoed so much.

Two hours had past before Dixon found what he was looking for. A folder wrapped with an elastic band laid right at the bottom of the box. Photos were clipped to each file and this one looked a lot like Jasmine. As he opened the file he was met with a brief description of the little girl and what happened.
'At 10:15am, young Jasmine Halt was snatched from her push chair as her mother attended to her younger daughter who had hurt herself.
Mollie Halt and Andrew Half noticed no strangers around either of their daughters.
The investigation has been left open but suspended due to no leads.'

This was it. He'd found her. He must have. He took the file and raced back to his own office leaving the archive room in a state. As he left he shouted at the all,
"I'll clear it up later" and he made his way up the stairs back to the major crime unit. He hurled his way into his office to find Jasmine still sitting in the seat he'd left her in.
"I need a photo of when you were younger" Jasmine reaches for her phone and found a photo from around eighteen years ago on Facebook. Dixon looked at the photo on the file and on Jasmines phone and left once again, staring at both. He was greeted by Sarah who was sitting at her desk.
"I need contact details for Mollie and Andrew Halt. I have their daughter. Tell them to come in" again, he left staring at the two photos. Making comparisons between the two. They were definitely the same person. The birthdays matched, the account Mrs Walters

had given to Jasmine added up. It all fell into place. He sat opposite Jasmine and let out a smile. A great big smile that showed off his perfectly straight but coffee stained teeth. "We found them. Your real parents. I've asked Sarah to call them so they can come in. We'll need a DNA test to make sure but the birthdays and photos add up" Dixon was still smiling. Jasmine however, wasn't. Emotions yet again engulfed her body and doubt started to enter her mind. She looked up at Dixon for the first time since he'd sat down. "But... what if they don't like me. How did they not notice I was gone?" Dixon's smile started to fade, he didn't know all of the answers but he showed Jasmine the file he had in this hands. He slid it across the table and Jasmine started reading the brief description Dixon had read himself only moments before. For the first time in a long time, a smile slowly crept along Jasmines face. Her heard pounding fast and excitement raged through her body. She was loved.

Sarah entered the officer door and looked at Dixon who nodded as if to say, 'she knows, go ahead'.
"I phoned them. I only got through to Mollie because Andrew seems to be at work but she's on her way in. She'll be maybe twenty minutes" Sarah left the room, leaving Dixon and Jasmine smiling proudly at each other. He'd helped to solve and crime and Jasmine and her real family back. He'd brought Jasmine just a tad of justice, the rest would come from solving these murders. However, that wasn't going to be an easy task. These two murders, these two victims weren't tied together in any obvious path which subsequently meant that the whole team would have to do some serious digging. For now though, any answers Dixon could get would be from the interviews.

Chapter Seven

The interviews begun just how Dixon thought they would, in silence. Mr Walters sat there looking at the floor having been advised by his solicitor not to say anything. Mrs Walters sat staring at the interviewer, a fierce woman with short black hair and a silk shirt, whilst giving a small and sinister grin that again, only presented itself at one corner of her mouth. It had been maybe thirty minutes before Mr Walters said anything at all, his ego just wouldn't let him stay quiet for much longer.
"I don't understand why you've roped me into this when it's my so called wife you should be questioning. I have nothing to do with any of this. Ask my daughter. She'll tell you. Ask Jasmine!" The interviewer, who was a middle aged man with blonde hair and glasses, smiled at him.
"Mr Walters, you're hear on suspicion of murder, kidnapping and harassment. It was your *so called* daughter who handed you in. We have footage of you this morning at the station. We tracked your movements. Why hand in a photo of you missing daughter when you hugged her that same day. Why leave a not for her to find before you left and then an hour later, get your neighbour to knock on the door. We have the phone records too" the interviewer tilted his head in satisfaction. He'd got him right where he wanted him. Mr Walters couldn't say anything. He knew they'd have enough evidence. Why bother. So he did what everyone thought he wouldn't do, he owned up to it all. He confessed to everything. To the killings, to kidnapping and to harassment. His wife however, no so easy. She was cunning. Mrs Walters knew that a half hearted confession to her emotional daughter wasn't enough for them to charge her, she just had to stay quiet.

After another hour, Mr Walters was realised from the interview room but was held in a cell for another hour whilst a transfer request was put in. Mrs Walters on the other hand, she was let home due to insufficient evidence. Little did they know, this is what the two of them had been planning all along.

Mrs Walters made her way home, she flopped onto the floor in the most dramatic way possible and managed to cut her arm in the process. She looked at her arm, smiled again and touched it with her index finger which left blood trickling down her arm and onto her white shirt. She made her way slowly into the kitchen, staggering like she was drunk and slid her hand into the knife draw. She grabbed the largest and scariest knife in the draw before sliding into her bag and leaving again in her black *Range Rover.*

Mr Walters' transfer had finally been granted and within minutes, he was in handcuffs and onto a police van. Moments later, two full sized trucks pulled up and pounded the police van until it was on its side and all the windows had been smashed. From each truck, one man climbed out of the cab. One of the men shot the police officers with a gun that had a silencer on the end, the other had started to drag Mr Walters out of the van and set him free. It was only five minutes before Mr Mark Walters was free. Free to cause havoc.

After thirty minutes Mark and the four men pulled up at an abounded warehouse, Mark Walters walked in a smiled. He looked at the four boys and patted the two next to him on the shoulder.
"Well done boys" Stood in front of him was a large circus tent decorated in banners and lights. Red and yellow stripes made the tent look colourful and happy but inside was a very unhappy setting. Mrs Walters then arrived and drove her car into the warehouse. Two

of the men, who looked like bodybuilders, shut the doors to the warehouse and bolted them shut. Mrs Walters walked over to her husband who smiled at her.

"Darling" mark put his arm around his wife and walked her into the tent. What greeted them next was a horrific site. Sat in each bench were at least four corpses. Sixteen people of all ages sat dead facing the centre ring. No performers. A spot was free in the ring, a pink sequinned leotard and skirt lay on the floor which was obviously free for Jasmine. But how would they find their performer?

Mark Walters walked through the crowd of bodies. His arms in the air and his wife standing by one side with a scary grin spread across her face. Her hand holding each other, placed just by her face as she rested her chin on the fist it made.

"WELCOME!!!" A booming voice rang through the tent. Mark grabbed a top hat and flipped it onto his head, taking a bow he grabbed a cane which he rested on.

"Unfortunately our ring master could not join us this evening. Nor could our security guard, but soon, hopefully we'll have our performer..." claps and cheers rang through the audience which left Mark smiling. In his head, everyone sitting there was clapping and throwing roses into the ring. In reality, it stayed silent. All of the corpses in the room were placed perfectly so they all faced the ring, all tied with rope and tape, some even had flowers and brochures in their hands. Mark took a bow as if he'd finished an act, one they loved.

"My wife brought us all together. She held us all and in this tough time whilst we get our performer back, we should all thank her for the effort she made" Mark held out his hand and took a bow as his wife, Patricia made her way towards the ring and stood hand in hand with her husband. Of course, just like Mark, Patricia Walters could hear and see the audience cheering and clapping, but of course, reality proved wrong.

"Please. Stay seated. We'll offer refreshments whilst we fill our performer position. Hopefully there should be little to no wait. Enjoy!" Patricia smiled that menacing smile and clapped as her husband left the tent, she was ushering all the bodies in the room to do the same. She sighed, smiled and left too.

Chapter Eight

A twenty minute wait seemed to feel like forever. Who knew that the longest wait Jasmine would ever have, would be the most important. Butterflies seemed to occupy her stomach and a headache started to present itself as she eagerly awaited her mother. The real one. *'Halt'*. That one word seemed to be swirling around her head. She kept repeating it. That was *her* name. The real one. Finally, after all the waiting Jasmine had done, there was a knock at the door. Her heart dropped from her chest, all the way to her feet and suddenly, she wasn't so excited. Dixon walked over to the door, took a look back at jasmine and opened it. Stood at the door was this woman, younger than Jasmine had expected. Long blonde hair swept passed her shoulders. A kind and warming face stood looking at Jasmine. Nobody knew what to do next. No words were muttered for the next minute, just silence. Jasmine had no idea what to do next. Then, Mollie swept forward and grabbed her daughter, both arms tightly bound around Jasmine. They both breathed a sigh of content and Jasmine relaxed enough to be able to hug her back.

After another thirty minutes, Mollie and Jasmine were finally left alone. They both looked at each other. Both had been given mounds of information on what happened now but neither had really taken anything in. Both had questions. Mollie spoke first much to Jasmine's delight, she was far too nervous.
"How's life been for you?" Mollie had an Australian accent. Strong but not harsh.
"Good. Ish... well, it was good for a while. Australian?" Jasmine didn't know how much her mum knew, how much she didn't know. What she thought of her.
"Yeah. I grew up in Australia until I was around twenty, then met your dad and moved here. You went missing when you were just under one. I hate myself for that day, I left you whilst I saw to Charlotte in the other buggy. I should have paid more attention to you" tears started to fall from Mollie's face. Jasmine suddenly felt the urge to hug her, not something she felt before. She leaned in and grabbed Mollie tight and spoke calmly and softly to her.
"I don't blame you for that that. Everything happens for a reason" suddenly, all of Jasmine's life made sense. Everything that had happened or even, everything that was going to, was meant to happen. What jasmine said helped Mollie. The tears started to fade and a smile lit up her face.

Mark was closing in. He'd hatched a cunning plan earlier in the day when he first arrived at the police station. He was meant to get caught. He knew exactly what he was doing. He wasn't stupid though, Mark kept to the speed limit and made sure he took rural roads to avoid cameras. There was no way he was getting caught now. After a thirty minute drive, Mark arrived outside the old house, the drove straight past and parked the car five minutes away from the house. He walked inside, he was ready.

Mollie and Jasmine decided they wanted to go and get some things so they could set off. Jasmine was desperate to go home and forget about everything that had happened. Just after they'd left the station, Sarah came flying into Dixon's office and almost fell onto his desk.
"GONE! He's gone. Mark Walters. He managed to escape, killing three officers in the process" Sarah looked around Dixon's office and then back at him.
"Where's Mollie and Jasmine?" Dixon shot up from his chair, grabbed his keys and raced out of his office door.

"Call for back up to the Walters house!" Dixon drove at 40mph In a twenty zone to get through to Jasmine and Mollie. He'd switched the sirens off but the lights were still flashing. He didn't want to let Mark know he was on his way.

When Dixon entered the Walter house, he found blood splatters across the walls, tables and chairs knocked over and behind the sofa, he could see a small slither of shiny blonde hair. Dixon approached slowly, he didn't know what he'd find but he hoped and willed it not to be Mollie. Then, to his amazement, it was Mollie, but she was alive. Her eyes were wide and her mouth and hands were taped. Dixon took the tape off Mollie's face and wiped the tears away from her cheeks.
"He took her. That man, he took Jasmine. She's gone again" Mollie again, started crying.
"Back up is on the way. Do you know where they went" Mollie pointed to a poster that was laying on the floor. It looked old, tea stained paper like the designs from primary school. A photo of a tent and bold letters advertising a circus made up the majority of the page. Dixon grabbed the paper and ran out of the door. He sped off in his car.

It was again, thirty minutes before Dixon reached the warehouse. No sirens at all this time, not even lights. Dixon shuffled out of his car and left the drivers door open. What he'd find next, was something he'd never even imagine he'd see. The warehouse doors were left open, like they were expecting him. Patricia was stood at the tent door ushering in imaginary spectators, she didn't even notice the DCI. He walked in to find bodies sitting in the benches, a lot of the missing people he'd seen on the posters earlier were here. The elderly, men, teens, women and children. All dead. All sitting watching an imaginary show. Mark was turning 360 degrees on the spot. His arms in the air. The cane in one hand and the top hat still placed perfectly on his head. Jasmine was in her outfit by this time, taped to the chair and her hands bound with rope behind her. She saw Dixon enter but Mark and Patricia could only hear and see a mound of imaginary spectators ready to watch their show.

"MARK!" Dixon shouted across the centre ring but by this time, Dixon found it obvious that he couldn't hear him. He mouthed to jasmine.
"Perform. Then run to me" Jasmine nodded and Dixon took his seat. The show was about to begin.
Mark stood facing everyone, he help up his arms again and swung the cane around in the air.
"Ladies and Gents. I will be filling in for ring master. You've joined us today to watch Jasmine here perform her world renowned act. So scary, so tricky, she may not survive. Watch, as she performs!" Mark then untied her from the chair she was bound to. Gripped her arm tightly and swung her over to the rope at the front of the ring. Jasmine looked over to DCI Dixon and started to tear up. He nodded, she ran. She ran faster than she ever did and straight into Dixon's arms. He hugged her so tightly she could feel her lungs being squashed. Mark pointed his cane over to them and a great booming voice sounded.
"STOP THEM" Dixon and Jasmine knew this was their only chance to turn and run, they ran straight for the exit and towards the warehouse doors. Jasmine was thrown into Dixon's car and Dixon slammed the door shut. Mark and Patricia were running towards the car just as Dixon locked the car tightly. Mark grabbed Dixon by the collar and slammed him into the side of the car. Patricia Walters was on the other side of the car banging at the window. Blood was being smeared down the side of it as Patricia stood there with a grin on her face showing blood stained teeth. Her mascara was smudged and had run down her face all the way to her chin. Jasmine couldn't do anything but watch as Dixon was being hurt. Then she noticed the car radio. She called it in, she told

the operator everything that was happening and within five minutes, four other cars turned up. Around ten officers raced out of their cars and over to the DCI who was now on the floor with one arm forced behind his back whilst Mark smashed his head into the ground. Blood seeped out of a wound from his forehead and Dixon was now screaming in agony from his arm. Patricia had to be pulled away by three strong officers. Blood was now trickling down the window by Jasmine. She was prised away from the car but not before she could grab a knife from her pocket and smash the window leaving several small abrasions on Jasmine's face. She started stabbing the knife at Jasmine through the window but managed to scrape one of the officers instead.

Chapter Nine

Mollie was standing beside Andrew and Charlotte waiting for Jasmine to be discharged. The hospital lights were bright and warming whilst outside, it was the dead of night. Doctors were rushing around attending to alarms, screaming patients and drunks who were causing havoc. Dixon had just finished being patched up when he made his way into Jasmine's cubical. He had stitches across his forehead just above his eyebrow and his right arm in a cast. He seemed relieved. It was all over.
"How's the arm?" Jasmine couldn't help but feel guilty at the thought that she'd caused his injury, she felt as though the should have acted quicker.
"It's fine. It'll heal" by this time, Sarah had also made her way into the hospital and joined them all. She smiled as she closed the case file for good with a brown elastic band which had the reference number written on it.

After another ten minutes doctors finally discharged Jasmine. A mound of rope burns loomed on her wrists and a few stitches on her leg meant she was on crutches for a while. She was just grateful to be home with her *real* family. Mollie couldn't help but smile and she held Jasmine's hand and hugged Charlotte tightly around her shoulders. Andrew was on the other side of Jasmine's bed flicking through his phone, looking up every so often at his family. He walked over to the end of Jasmine's bed and got the three of them to pose for a photo so he could post it on Facebook.
'She's home' the caption read along with a photo of the three girls. Dixon just looked on and smiled as he saw how loving the family was, he knew he'd helped to bring them all back together.

Sarah's phone started to ring, she looked at her phone and took the call outside in the cold. After five minutes she yet again, came rushing through the double doors and found herself having to lean onto the counter for support.
"Sarah. What is it?" Dixon rushed over to her just as a doctor did too. Sarah waved her hand as if to brush them away. Both Dixon and the doctor took a step back but the Halt family were also watching every move.
"It wasn't him...." she took a few more deep breaths before talking again. This time, with ease.
"The sixteen bodies they found, he didn't kill them. We found encrypted files on Patricia's computer, she bought them online. He didn't kill Graham or the other man either. The killer is still out there" Silence filled the room. Andrew Halt grabbed his family right as Dixon spun around and took a long hard sorry look at them. Dixon mouthed the word 'sorry' to Jasmine but he could tell on her face, nothing could be done or said to make the fear she had in her body disappear.

Jasmine, Mollie, Sarah and DCI Dixon all stood in the IT suit watching the video footage of the confession. Sure enough, there it was. Mark Walters had confessed to kidnapping among others, Patricia Halt again, had confessed to kidnapping among others but presented on the next screen over were conversations between Patricia and the seller. The IT technician brought up CCTV footage from the warehouse and then they saw it. Another man and woman bringing in the sixteen bodies found in the tent. The killers were still out there and Dixon knew, nobody was safe.

About the author:

Amelia Harris is originally from Lewisham in South London. Through her nineteen years, she's moved up and down the England.
From a young age she looked up to authors and would write pages and pages, making up her own stories.
Now, at nineteen, Amelia has decided to take her love of books further by publishing this book for everyone to read and enjoy.

Printed in Great Britain
by Amazon